SHERLOCK HOLMES

THE ENGINEER'S THUMB

SIR ARTHUR CONAN DOYLE

THE
SHERLOCK
HOLMES

CHILDREN'S COLLECTION

MYSTERY, MISCHIEF
AND MAYHEM

Published by Sweet Cherry Publishing Limited
Unit 36, Vulcan House,
Vulcan Road,
Leicester, LE5 3EF
United Kingdom

First published in the UK in 2020
2020 edition

2 4 6 8 10 9 7 5 3 1

ISBN: 978-1-78226-423-1

© Sweet Cherry Publishing

Sherlock Holmes: The Engineer's Thumb

Based on the original story from Sir Arthur Conan Doyle,
adapted by Stephanie Baudet.
Cover design by Arianna Bellucci and Rhiannon Izard
Illustrations by Arianna Bellucci

www.sweetcherrypublishing.com

Printed and bound in China
C.WM004

Only twice have I been able to give my friend, Sherlock Holmes, a problem to solve. The mystery of Mr Hatherley's thumb was one of them.

The story took place in the summer of 1889, not long after Mary and I got married. As well as being married, I was opening my own doctor's surgery. I had moved out of Baker Street, but I

still visited Holmes quite often.
He visited us too, once or twice,
though he really did not enjoy
the dinner parties, or the tea
parties, or any type of party
we had.

As I lived near Paddington
Station, a few of the people who
worked there were my patients.
One train guard was so grateful for
my help that he told all his friends
and family to come and see me, too.

One morning, at a little before

seven o'clock, the maid
knocked on my bedroom door.
She told me that two men from
Paddington Station were waiting
in my doctor's office. I dressed
quickly and ran downstairs.

7

I knew that any accident that happened at the station could be serious.

As I came down the stairs, I saw the train guard who liked me so much come out of my office. He closed the door behind him.

'I've got him in here,' he whispered in a strangely excited voice. He pointed his thumb over his shoulder and then flinched away from the door. 'He's all right.'

'What is it, then?' I asked, a little confused. His odd behaviour made me think he had a dangerous animal caged up in my room.

'It's a new patient,' he whispered, sounding even more excited than before. You would have thought by his tone that he had brought me an expensive present, not a patient to attend to. 'I thought I'd bring him round myself. He's here, all safe and sound. I must go now, Doctor. I have my duties, just like you.' And off he went without even giving me time to thank him.

I walked into my office and found a gentleman sitting by the table. He was dressed in a light tweed suit. He had taken his cap off his head and laid it on top of a pile of my books. There was a handkerchief wrapped around one of his hands. It was covered in blood.

The gentleman was young – not more than twenty-five. He had a strong, manly face, but was very pale. From the look in his eyes, I could tell he had had a horrible fright.

'I am sorry to get you up so early, Doctor,' he said. 'But I have had a very serious accident in the night. I came in by train this morning. When I asked for the nearest doctor, a train guard kindly brought me here. I gave the maid my card, but I see she has left it on the side table.'

I picked it up and read it.

MR VICTOR HATHERLEY
Hydraulic Engineer,
16a Victoria Street
(3rd floor),
London

'I am sorry I kept you waiting,'
I said, sitting down in my
chair. 'You must be very tired.
Especially after a long, boring
train journey.'

'Oh, my journey could not be
called boring,' Mr Hatherley
said, and laughed. He laughed
very loudly, leaning back in his
chair and shaking, with his eyes
firmly closed. It seemed as if he
could not stop. It was strange
laughter, and it worried me.

13

'Calm down!' I said. I poured him some water from a jug and handed it to him.

But it didn't help. He was caught in a fit of giggles. In my experience, these fits often happen after a crisis. They are a sort of reaction to the shock. At last, Mr Hatherley calmed down. His cheeks turned a deep red.

'I have been making a fool of myself,' he said.

'Not at all. Drink this.' I put a

little medicine into his water glass.
He took a few sips and relaxed.

'That's better,' he said. 'Now,
Doctor, can you help me with
my thumb? Or, really, the place
where my thumb used to be.'

He took off the handkerchief
and held out his hand. It was
a horrible sight. Even though I
had been an army doctor,
it made me shudder to
look at it. Next to
his four fingers

15

there was a horrid red, spongy surface, where his thumb should have been.

'Good heavens!' I cried. 'This is a terrible injury! It must have bled a lot.'

'Yes, it did. I fainted when it happened. I didn't wake up for a long time, and even when I did, it was still bleeding. I tied my handkerchief very tightly around my wrist and held my arm above my head.'

'Excellent work! You should have been a surgeon.'

'It's a question of engineering, you see,' said Mr Hatherley. 'I'm an expert in it.'

I examined the wound. 'This has been done by something very heavy and very sharp.'

'Something like a butcher's cleaver,' Mr Hatherley said.

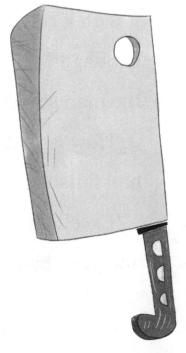

'An accident?' I asked.

'No, not at all.'

'What! A deadly attack, then?'

'Very deadly.'

'You horrify me!' I cried.

I cleaned the injury and covered it with a cotton dressing and bandage. While I was working, the man stayed oddly calm.

'How is that?' I asked when I had finished.

'Excellent! With your medicine and your bandage, I feel like a new man. I was very weak. It was such a horrible night.'

'Maybe you should not speak about it,' I said. 'It is clearly upsetting you.'

'Oh, no,' Mr Hatherley replied, 'I shall have to tell my tale to the police. It's such a strange tale, though. If I didn't have this horrible wound, I don't think the police would believe it. Apart from my bleeding hand, I don't have any proof of what happened.

And even if they do believe me, I do not think I can help them solve the mystery. I have a few clues, but they are so odd that I don't think they will help at all.'

'Ha!' I cried. 'If you have a problem that needs solving, you should ask my friend, Mr Sherlock Holmes. Go to him before you go to the police.'

'Oh, I have heard of that fellow,' said Mr Hatherley. 'I would be very happy if he would help. Though,

I must tell the police as well. Can you introduce me to Mr Holmes?'

'I will take you to see him right now.'

'That would be very kind.'

'We'll call a cab. We shall just be in time to have breakfast with him. Do you feel up to it?' I asked.

The man was looking much better than when he arrived.

'Yes. And I will feel even better once I've told my tale,' Mr Hatherley replied.

'Then my maid will call a cab. I will be back in one moment.'

I ran upstairs and told my wife where we were going. Five minutes later we were inside a cab, driving to Baker Street.

Sherlock Holmes was, as I expected, relaxing in his sitting room. He was wearing his dressing gown and reading *The Times*.

'Watson! So good to see you!'
Holmes looked curiously at Mr
Hatherley. Then he smiled and
asked us to sit down.

'This is Mr Hatherley,' I said. 'He
came to me this morning with a
horrible injury. He has a problem
to solve. I told him to come to you.'

Holmes nodded. I could not
read the look on his face. I did not
know whether he was interested,
or annoyed at me for bringing Mr
Hatherley to him.

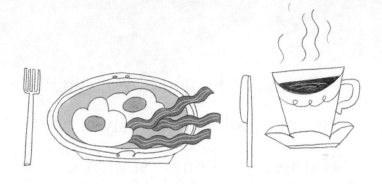

'Will you join me for breakfast?' Holmes asked. He rang the bell for Mrs Hudson, the housekeeper.

We all had a tasty meal of bacon, eggs and coffee. Then Holmes sat Mr Hatherley on the sofa. He put a pillow under his head and a glass of medicine and water beside him. I was surprised at how caring he was being.

'It is easy to see that your story is not a nice one, Mr Hatherley,' he said. 'Please lie down there and make yourself at home. Tell us what you can, but stop when you are tired. The medicine should help keep your strength up.' He pointed to the drink.

'Thank you,' said Hatherley, 'but I have felt much better since the doctor bandaged me. I think your breakfast has completed the cure. I shall take up as little of your time as possible. Let me begin my story.'

Holmes sat in his big armchair. He pressed his fingertips together, as he often did when he thought the case would be interesting. I sat opposite him. We listened in silence to the strange story.

'You must know,' Mr Hatherley said, 'that I'm an orphan and I'm not married. I live alone in a flat, in London. By profession, I am a hydraulic engineer. I was an apprentice for seven years, at a Greenwich firm called Venner & Matheson.

'Two years ago, I finished my apprenticeship. At the same time, my father died. He left me a lot of money, so I decided to set up my own business. I rented some rooms in Victoria Street, to be my office.

Hydraulic engineer

This is a very skilled job. Hydraulic machines use water to work. For instance, a stamping machine would use the pressure made by releasing a huge flow of water, to push the stamp down. A hydraulic engineer works to build, care for and repair these machines.

'Most people must find starting a business very tricky. I did. I started two years ago, but I have only had three meetings and one small job. I've only made twenty-seven pounds and ten shillings. Every day, from nine o'clock until four, I waited in my little office. Until, at last, my heart began to sink. I didn't think I would ever have any work.

'Yesterday, however, I was just about to leave the office when my assistant came in. He said that there was a gentleman waiting for me. The assistant gave me his card. It had "Colonel Lysander Stark" written on it.

'Then the colonel himself walked into the room. He was quite tall and extremely thin. I don't think I have ever seen such a thin man. He had a sharp face, with a pointy nose and chin. This thinness seemed natural to him. He did not seem to be ill or

unhealthy. His eyes were bright and his walk was quick. He was probably nearer forty than thirty years old.

"'Mr Hatherley?" he asked, with a slight German accent. "I have heard you are a very clever and very skilled man. And that you can keep a secret.'"

The word 'secret' made Holmes open his eyes. He stared at our visitor.

Hatherley stopped for a moment.

'Please continue,' said Holmes. 'This is such an interesting story.'

'Well, I bowed at the thin man. I felt very flattered. I think anyone would. "Can I ask who said these nice things about me?" I asked the colonel.

'"It might be better if I do not tell you that. I also know that you have no parents and no wife. You are living alone in London."

"'That is correct," I answered. "But I do not see how this makes me any better or worse at my job. I thought you wanted to speak to me about business."

"'I do," he replied. "But these facts are important. I have a job for you, but you must keep it a complete secret. You cannot tell anyone. It will be easier because you have no family to tell."

'"*If* I promise to keep the secret," I said, "then I will keep it forever."

'He looked very hard at me as he spoke. I had never seen someone look at me that way. It was as if he were trying to read my thoughts.

'"You do promise then?" he asked at last.

'"Yes, I promise."

'"You'll keep it a complete secret? Even after you've finished the job? You won't write anything about it, or speak about it?"

"'I already gave you my word."

"'Very good," the man said, with a nod. Then he suddenly sprang up from his chair. Darting like lightning across the room, he pulled open the door and peered into the hallway. It was empty.

"'That's all right," he said, coming back to his chair.

"I just wanted to check that your assistant wasn't there. Now we can talk safely." The colonel pulled his chair very close to mine and started to stare at me again.

'I began to feel a little scared of this colonel and his strange job offer. Even though I did not want to lose the man as a client, I could not help looking impatient. He was taking far too long to get to the point.

'"Please tell me about the job, sir," I said. "My time is valuable."

'That last sentence was hardly true, but I said it anyway.

'"Would fifty guineas for one night's work be all right?" he asked.

'"That would be very good," I replied.

'"I say a night's work, but it will probably only be one hour. I have a hydraulic stamping machine that is not working. If you show me what is wrong with it, we shall soon fix it ourselves.

What do you think of that?"

"'The job seems easy and the pay seems very good.'"

"'Excellent. We will want you to come tonight, by the last train.'"

"'Where to?'"

"'To Eyford, in Berkshire. It is a little place near the border of Oxfordshire, close to Reading. There is a train from Paddington Station that will get you to Eyford at eleven-fifteen.'"

"'Very good,' I said, nodding.

"'I shall come down in a carriage to meet you.'

"'It's not near the station then?'

"'No, our little place is out in the country. It is a good seven miles from Eyford station.'

"'But then we won't get there before midnight. I won't be able to get a train back. I would have to stay the night.'

"'Yes, that won't be a problem.'

"'It is a problem for me. Couldn't I come earlier in the day?'

'"No. We thought it best that you should come late. We are paying you a lot of money to do so. Still, of course, you can back out of the job."

'I thought of the fifty guineas. The money would be very useful to me.

'"Not at all," I said. "I shall be happy to do as you ask. I would like, however, to know a little more about what you want me to do."

"'Of course. It is natural that by telling you to keep it a secret, you are now very curious. I will tell you everything you need to know. Are you absolutely sure that no one can hear us?"

"'Absolutely.'"

"'Then here it is. You probably know that fuller's earth is a valuable product? It is only found in one or two places in England."

"'I have heard so, yes.'"

"'Some time ago I bought a

very small place within ten miles of Reading. I was lucky enough to find some fuller's earth in one of my fields. When I looked closer, however, I found that there was only a very small amount. The fuller's earth in my field actually links two larger lots of fuller's earth to the right and to the left.

Fuller's earth

Fuller's earth is a clay soil that can absorb oils and grease, and remove unwanted colours. It is often used to clean wool before it is made into clothing, and is prized by people in the textiles industry. Finding a patch of fuller's earth on your land could make you very rich, indeed.

But both of the large areas were in my neighbour's land.

"'They did not know that their land contained something as valuable as a gold mine. I planned to buy their land before they found out, but I had no money. So I told a few of my friends about the fuller's earth. They said if we secretly dug out some of it from our little patch, we could sell it. Then we could get enough money to buy the land.

'"We have been doing this for some time. That's why we needed the hydraulic press. This press, as I said, is not working. We want your advice, so we can fix it. But we can't let the neighbours know what we are doing. If they saw that we had a hydraulic engineer coming to our house, they would ask questions. Then the secret would come out and I could never buy the fields off them. That is why I made you promise not to tell anyone. Does that make sense?"

'"Yes," I said. '"The only thing I don't understand is how you use a hydraulic press. How can that help you to dig fuller's earth out of the ground?"

'"Ah!" the colonel replied. "We have our own special way. We press the earth into bricks. Then we can take the bricks out of the ground without showing the neighbours what they are.

But that is not important. I have told you everything now, Mr Hatherley. I have shown you that I trust you."

'He stood up as he spoke. "I will see you at Eyford then, at eleven-fifteen."

'"I will be there."

'"And do not say a word to anyone," he said, staring at me again. He wrapped his cold fingers around my hand and shook it. Then he hurried from the room.

'I just couldn't get my head around it. Why had this secret, well-paid job suddenly come to me? On the one hand, I was glad. The money was at least ten times what I would have asked for. Plus, it might lead to more jobs.

'But, the man's face, and his cold, strange speech had sent shivers down my spine. I didn't believe his story about fuller's earth. And I still didn't understand why I had to travel there at midnight, and never tell anyone.

'I ignored my fears, though. After a big dinner I drove to Paddington Station and got on the train.'

Holmes and I were leaning forward in our chairs. We were hooked by the story.

'At Reading,' went on Hatherley, 'I had to change my train. Well, not just my train, but change station, too. I was just in time to catch the last train to Eyford. I reached the little dimly-lit station after eleven o'clock. I was the only passenger to get off there. There was no one on the platform except a sleepy porter with a lantern.

'When I stepped through the gate, I saw the colonel waiting in the shadows. Without a word, he pulled my arm and hurried me into a carriage. He closed the curtains across the windows. Then he tapped on the woodwork, and the carriage set off as fast as the horse could go.'

'One horse?' interrupted Holmes.

'Yes, only one,' replied Mr Hatherley.

'Did you notice the colour?'

'Yes, I saw it as I stepped in. It was chestnut brown.'

'Tired-looking or fresh?'

'Oh, fresh and glossy.'

Holmes leaned back a little. 'Thank you. I'm sorry to interrupt you. Please go on.'

Hatherley took a deep breath and I checked him over with my eyes. His colour was good, though he did look tired. His thumb, at least, had stopped bleeding.

'We drove for at least an hour,' he said. 'The colonel had said that it was only seven miles, but it felt more like twelve.

'The colonel sat silently the whole time. He was staring at me a lot, barely looking away. The country roads seemed to be very poor in Eyford. The carriage shook and jolted all the time. I tried to look out of the windows

to see where we were, but they were made of frosted glass. I could see nothing except for a few blurs of passing light.

'Now and then I tried to break the silence. I asked the colonel questions, but he only grunted in reply. At last, the bumpy roads stopped. The carriage moved onto a smooth gravel drive, before stopping completely. Colonel Lysander Stark sprang out and I followed after him. He pulled me swiftly into a porch in front of us and straight into the hallway of a house. I did not get one look at the outside of the building. As soon as we walked through the front door, the colonel slammed it behind us. I heard the carriage's wheels rattle as it drove away.

'It was pitch dark inside the house. The colonel fumbled about looking for matches and muttering under his breath. Suddenly, a door opened at

the other end of the hall. A
long, golden bar of light shone
through it. The ray of light
grew bigger and bigger. It was
a woman holding a lamp above
her head. She was walking
towards us, staring at me. When
the light shone on her dress
I could see that it was a rich,
glossy material. She said a few
words in a language I didn't
understand. I could tell she was
asking questions though.

The colonel answered
with one gruff, short
word. Then the
lady jumped with
shock. She nearly
dropped the lamp.

'Colonel Stark
did not look
happy. He walked
up to her and
whispered something
in her ear. Then he
snatched the lamp from

her and pushed her back into the room she had come out of. He walked back to me with the lamp in his hand.

'"Would you wait here for a moment, please?" he asked. He threw open another door and showed me into a room. It was a quiet, plain little room. It had a round table in the centre,  with several German books on top of it. Colonel Stark put

56

the lamp on top of a small piano, next to the door. "I will be back very soon," he said, and vanished into the darkness.

'I looked at the books on the table. I do not speak German, but I could see that two of the books were about science and the others were about poetry. I walked across to the window. I hoped I might be able to see the countryside, but a heavy wooden shutter sat over the window.

'The house was so quiet. There was an old clock ticking loudly somewhere in the hallway. Other than that, everything was deadly still. I felt a little nervous suddenly. Who were these people, and what were they doing living in this strange place? What on earth was this place? I was ten miles or so from Eyford, I knew that. But I had no idea if we were to the north, south, east or west. The colonel said we were near

Reading. Yet I was sure, from the stillness and silence, that we were in the countryside.

'I paced up and down the room, humming a tune. I was trying to stay positive. I had to do this; I had to earn my fifty guineas.

'Suddenly and silently the door of the room opened. The woman was standing in the doorway, holding a lamp. She looked frightened. The sight sent a chill to my heart.

'She held up one shaking finger to her lips, telling me to be quiet. Then she began to speak.

'"I would go," she said, in a strong accent. She was trying hard to speak calmly. "I would go. Do not stay here. There is no good for you to do."

'"But madam," I said, "I have not finished the job I came to do.

I cannot leave until I have seen the hydraulic machine."

"'No, you should not wait," she went on. "You can pass through the door. No one will stop you." I smiled and shook my head. Seeing this, she suddenly stepped forward and pressed her hands together. "For the love of heaven," she whispered. "Leave before it is too late!"'

Mr Hatherley paused again. He seemed to be reliving the moment in his head. He needed to calm himself down.

'I am quite stubborn,' he continued. 'When someone says I cannot do something, I want to do it even more. I thought of my fifty-guinea payment. I also thought about my tiring journey. Was all my effort going to be for nothing? Why should I slip away without doing the job and getting the money? Was this woman even telling the truth?

'Although what she said had made me nervous, I shook my head again. I told her I was going to stay.

'She was about to speak again when a door slammed upstairs. I heard footsteps running down the stairs. The lady listened for a second. Then she threw her hands into the air and vanished into the darkness.

'Colonel Lysander Stark and a short, bearded man walked into

the room. The man's name was
Mr Ferguson.

"'This is my secretary and
my manager," said the colonel.
He looked at the door. "I
thought I'd left
this door shut.
I didn't
want a cold
draught
blowing in."

"'Actually," I
said, "I opened

the door myself. The room felt a little hot and stuffy."

'He shot me a questioning look. "We should get on with the business then," he said. "Mr Ferguson and I will take you up to see the machine."

'"I'd better put my hat on," I said, reaching for it.

'"Oh, no. The machine is in the house."

'"What? Do you dig fuller's earth in the house?"

'"No, no. This is only where we press the soil. But never mind that! All you have to do is look at the machine and tell us what is wrong with it."

'We walked upstairs together. The house was like a maze. It had corridors, passageways and narrow, winding staircases in every corner. We went through lots of small, low doorways. There were no carpets and no furniture above the first floor. Paint was peeling off the walls. Damp, mouldy patches stained the walls and floors. I tried to look calm, but I had not forgotten the lady's warnings.

I kept a keen watch on the two men. Mr Ferguson seemed like a quiet man. All I could tell was that he was English.

'At last, Colonel Lysander Stark stopped in front of a low door. He took a key and unlocked it. Inside was a small, square room. It was so

tiny, the three of us could hardly fit in. Mr Ferguson stayed outside, while the colonel showed me in.

"'We are now inside the hydraulic press," he said. "It would be

very nasty for us if anyone turned
the machine on. The ceiling of
this small room is actually the
end of the pressing block. It
comes down with a huge force
and slams onto this metal floor.
The machine goes well enough,
but it's a little stiff. Could you look
at it and show us how to fix it?"

'I took the lamp from him and
looked closely at the machine.
It was gigantic and looked very
powerful. I went outside and

pressed down the levers. I knew at once that there was a small leak.

'Looking closer, I saw that one of the rubber bands on the controls had shrunk. It was the reason the machine was not working properly. I pointed it out to the colonel. He listened very carefully and asked lots of questions.

'When I had explained everything, I went back into the tiny room and looked around.

It was such an interesting machine. It was clear, though, that it was not used for pressing fuller's earth. You would not need such a powerful machine for that.

'The walls of the little room were wooden, but the floor was iron. There were tiny pieces of metal all over it. I bent down to touch one. A loud shout came from behind me. I turned around to see the colonel looking down at me.

'"What are you doing?"
he asked.

'I felt angry at having been
tricked by his story about fuller's
earth. "I was admiring your
fuller's earth," I said, sarcastically.
"I would be able to help you more
if I knew what you *actually* use
the machine for."

'The second I said the words I
wished I had not. The colonel's face
hardened as if his skin had turned
to stone. I knew I was in danger.

'"Very well," he said. "You can know all about the machine." He took a step backwards and slammed the little door. I heard him turn the key in the lock. I pulled the handle and banged on the door. It didn't move!

'"Colonel! Let me out!"'

Mr Hatherley paused. He was breathing heavily. He tried to sit up, but I told him to lie back down. I couldn't imagine how scared he must have been, trapped in that tiny room.

Holmes had been holding his breath. He let it out in a sigh, then pressed his lips together and stared at Mr Hatherley.

'Suddenly, I heard a noise,' Hatherley said, with a shaky voice. 'The sound sent my heart to my mouth. I could not breathe. It was the clank of the levers. The colonel had switched on the engine!

'The lamp was still standing on the floor where I had put it. By its

light I saw that the black ceiling
was coming down on me. It
moved slowly, jerkily, but I knew
its force would grind me to a pulp
in less than a minute.'

I saw the terror in Mr
Hatherley's eyes.

'Oh, Mr Holmes. I threw
myself, screaming, at the door.
I tore my nails pulling at the
lock. I begged the colonel to let
me out, but the clanking noise
drowned my cries.

'Soon the ceiling was only a little way above my head. I pressed my hands against it, hard.

'Already, the ceiling was so low that I had to stand with my knees bent. I was sweating and shaking. But then I saw something that gave me a rush of hope.

'I saw a thin line of yellow light between two of the wooden boards of the walls. The line of light became bigger and bigger. It was a door! I could hardly believe it.

'I threw myself through the door. I landed on a hard floor and lay down, trying not to faint. The panel had closed again behind me. From the crash of the lamp and the clang of metal I could tell that I had escaped with only seconds to spare.

'I felt someone pulling at my wrist. When I opened my eyes I saw that I was lying on a stone floor in a narrow corridor. A woman was pulling at my arm with her left hand, and holding a candle in her right. It was the same woman who had warned me earlier.

'"Come! Come!" she cried. "They will be here in a moment. They will see that you are not dead. Oh, do not waste time. Come!"

'This time I did what she said. I stood up. We ran along the corridor and down a winding stairway. Just as we reached the next hallway, we heard the sound of running feet and two shouting voices.

'The woman stopped and looked around. She didn't know what to do. Then she threw open a door that led into a bedroom. It was brightly lit by moonlight shining through the window.

'"It is your only chance," she

said. "It is high, but you must jump out the window."

'As she spoke I saw the figure of Colonel Lysander Stark rushing through the hallway. He had a lantern in one hand, and a butcher's cleaver in the other.

'I rushed across the bedroom, flung open the window, and looked out. The garden did not look that far down.

'I climbed up onto the windowsill. I paused for a second.

I wanted to hear what the colonel
would say to the woman.
If he treated her badly,
then I would go back
to help her. The
thought had
hardly flashed
through
my mind
before he
was at the door.
He tried pushing
past her, but she

threw her arms around him to hold him back.

"'Fritz! Fritz!" she cried in English. "Remember your promise after the last time. You said it would not happen again. He will be silent! Oh, he will be silent!"

"'You are mad, Elise!" he shouted, struggling to break away from her. "He has seen too much. Let me pass!" He pushed her to one side and rushed to the window.

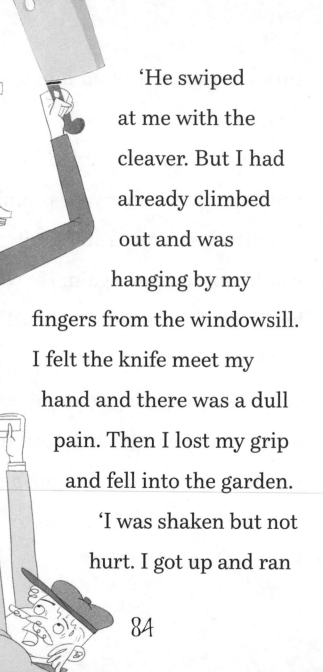

'He swiped
at me with the
cleaver. But I had
already climbed
out and was
hanging by my
fingers from the windowsill.
I felt the knife meet my
hand and there was a dull
pain. Then I lost my grip
and fell into the garden.

'I was shaken but not
hurt. I got up and ran

84

as fast as I could. I knew that I was not safe yet. As I ran, I started to feel dizzy and sick. I looked down at my hand, which was throbbing. I saw that my thumb had been cut off and blood was pouring from the wound. I tried to tie my handkerchief round it, but there was a sudden buzzing in my ears. The next moment I fainted and fell into the rose bushes.'

Hatherley looked down at his bandaged hand.

'Do you need something for the pain?' I asked, but he shook his head.

Holmes poured a little more water into his cup. Hatherley smiled and took a mouthful.

'I think you have almost finished your tale,' said Holmes. 'And I can already see the answer.'

This time, I had worked it out too.

Hatherley continued. 'I must have been lying in the rose

bushes for a long time. When I woke up the moon had gone and the sun was just coming up. My clothes were soaked with dew, and my coat sleeve was covered with blood. The pain from my hand made me remember what had happened in the night. I sprang to my feet. I was worried I might still be in danger. But, to my surprise, when I looked around I couldn't see the house or the garden. I was lying in the corner of a hedge, close to the main road. A little lower down the road was the same railway station I had arrived at the night before. If my thumb wasn't missing, I would have believed that it was all a horrible dream.

'I was very confused. I went to the station and asked about the morning train. There would be one to Reading in less than an hour.

The same porter was on duty as when I arrived.

'"Have you heard of a Colonel Lysander Stark?" I asked him. He had not. He had not noticed the carriage that had waited for me the night before, either.

'"Is there a police station nearby?" I asked.

'"About three miles away," he replied.

'I was too weak and ill to walk that far. So, I decided to wait until I got back to London before I told the police my story. It was just after six o'clock when I got to Paddington Station. That's when the train guard took me to see Dr Watson. Then the doctor was kind enough to bring me here.'

Mr Hatherley smiled at me. Then he turned to Holmes. 'I put the case into your hands. I will do everything you advise me to.'

We sat in silence for some time after listening to the story. Then

Holmes pulled a large book off the bookshelf.

'Look at this advert,' he said. 'It was printed in all the papers about a year ago.'

Lost on the 9th of this month. Mr Jeremiah Hayling, aged 26, a hydraulic engineer. He left his house at ten o'clock at night, and has not been heard from since. He was dressed in dark blue work trousers, a black jacket and a dark cloth cap.

'Ha!' said Holmes. 'That must be the last time that the colonel needed to have his machine fixed.'

'Good heavens!' cried Mr Hatherley. 'That explains what the woman said.' His face turned very pale.

Holmes nodded. 'It's quite clear that this colonel is a dangerous man. He doesn't want anyone or anything to stand in his way. Well, let's not waste any time. If you're up to it, Mr Hatherley, we will go down to Scotland Yard. Then we can head to Eyford.'

Three hours later we were all on the train, heading to the little village. Sherlock Holmes, Mr Hatherley, Inspector Bradstreet of Scotland Yard, a plain-clothed policeman and I were all ready

Plain-clothed policeman

When on the tail of a clever criminal, it is important not to scare them – if they think they are being followed by the police, they may run away before they can be arrested. A plain-clothed policeman wears normal clothing, rather than a uniform. Then, criminals cannot tell that they are being tracked by the police until the moment they close the handcuffs around their wrists.

for action. Inspector Bradstreet had a map of the area spread out on the table. He was using a compass to draw a circle, with Eyford at its centre.

'There you are,' he said. 'That circle shows

everything within ten miles of the village. The house we want must be somewhere near that line. You said it was a ten-mile drive, I think, sir?'

'It was a good hour's drive,' replied Hatherley.

'And you think that they brought you back to the main road after you fainted?'

'They must have. I do have some memory of being lifted up and taken somewhere.'

'I cannot understand why they let you live,' I said. 'Maybe the villain listened to the woman when she begged him not to kill you.'

'I don't think so,' said Hatherley. 'I never saw a meaner man in my life.'

'Well, we shall soon clear it all up,' said Bradstreet. 'I have drawn my circle. I just need to know exactly where the house is.'

'I could point my finger at it,' said Holmes.

I had noticed that he had been quiet while we were talking. He had a small, smug smile on his face. It made me smile, too. Of course, Holmes had it all worked out. He just loved watching others guess the wrong answers.

'Really now!' cried Bradstreet. 'You have your opinion. But let's see what everyone else thinks. I say it's south. The countryside is more deserted there.'

'And I say east,' said Mr Hatherley.

'I think west,' said the plain-clothed policeman. 'There are lots of quiet little villages up there.'

'I think it's in the north,' I said. 'There are no hills there, and our friend says that he did not notice the carriage go up any.'

'So,' said Bradstreet, laughing. 'Where do you think it is, Holmes?'

'You are all wrong,' Holmes replied.

'But we can't *all* be wrong,' said Bradstreet.

'Oh, yes you can. Here it is.' He placed his finger on the centre of the circle. 'This is where we shall find them.'

'But it was a ten-mile drive?' said Hatherley.

'They drove you five miles out and five miles back. It's simple. You said that the horse was fresh and glossy when you got into the carriage. How could it be, if it had travelled ten miles?'

'It could be true,' said Bradstreet. 'Of course, it's clear what these people do.'

'Very clear,' said Holmes. 'They are coiners on a large scale. They use the machine to make fake coins.'

'We have known for some time that a clever gang was at work,' said the inspector. 'They have been making thousands of half crowns. We tracked them as far as Reading, but we could never get any further. They covered their tracks very well. But now, thanks to this lucky

Coiners

These greedy criminals use machines to make fake money. Professional coiners can become very rich very quickly, but must keep their activities a complete secret, as making fake money is highly illegal. Some coiners will go to extreme lengths and even use violence to keep their money-making plans hidden from the eyes of the police.

chance, I think that we will catch them.'

But the inspector was wrong. When we arrived at Eyford station we saw a huge cloud of smoke coming from behind a small group of trees.

'Is a house on fire?' asked Bradstreet, as we stepped off the train.

'Yes, sir,' said the stationmaster.

'When did it start?'

'It was during the night, sir, but it has got worse. The whole place is on fire now.'

'Whose house is it?'

'Doctor Becher's.'

'Tell me,' said Hatherley, 'is Doctor Becher German? Is he very thin with a long, sharp nose?'

The stationmaster laughed heartily. 'No, sir, Doctor Becher is an Englishman. A very rich one. But he has a German gentleman staying with him. He's a patient, I think. And, yes, he does look like he could do with some good Berkshire beef.'

Hatherley nodded. 'That's the colonel all right.'

We left the stationmaster staring after us as we walked quickly towards the fire. We got to the top of a low hill and there was a huge white building in front of us. It had fire coming out of every corner and window. In the front garden there were three fire engines.

'That's it!' cried Hatherley. 'There is the gravel drive, and there are the rose bushes I fell into. That second window is the one I jumped out of.'

'Well, at least you have had your revenge,' said Holmes. 'When your oil lamp was crushed in the press it must have set fire to the wooden walls. The colonel was so focussed on chasing you that he didn't notice. Now keep your eyes open for the two men and the woman. Although, I think they are probably a hundred miles away by now.'

Holmes was right. To this day, no one has heard or seen anything of the kind woman, the dangerous German, or the quiet Englishman.

A farmer said that early that morning he saw a cart filled with a few people and some very bulky boxes.

It was driving quickly towards Reading. But after that, all traces of the criminals disappeared. Not even Holmes could find them.

The firemen had been very worried by the strange things they found inside the house. They were even more worried when they found a human thumb!

By sunset, they had managed to put the fire out. But the roof had fallen down and the whole house was destroyed. There was not even a trace left of the huge machine.

Large piles of nickel and tin were found in an outhouse, but there were no coins. I expect that is what was in the bulky boxes.

We would never have known how Mr Hatherley was carried from the garden to the road, if it weren't for the soil. There were two sets of footprints in the mud. One set was very small and one was very large. It was probably the silent Englishman. He was less bold and less violent than his German friend. He must have helped the kind woman to carry Mr Hatherley out of the way of danger.

'Well,' said the engineer, as we sat down on the train back to London. 'This has been a bad business for me! I have lost my thumb, and I have lost the fifty-guinea payment. And what have I gained?'

'A story,' said Holmes. 'You will have a good story to tell for the rest of your life.'

I was not sure that a good story made up for losing his thumb. But I was pleased that Holmes was looking on the bright side.

Sherlock Holmes

World-renowned private detective Sherlock Holmes has solved hundreds of mysteries, and is the author of such fascinating monographs as *Early English Charters* and *The Influence of a Trade Upon the Form of a Hand.* He keeps bees in his free time.

Dr John Watson

Wounded in action at Maiwand, Dr John Watson left the army and moved into 221B Baker Street. There he was surprised to learn that his new friend, Sherlock Holmes, faced daily peril solving crimes, and began documenting his investigations. Dr Watson also runs a doctor's practice.

To download Sherlock Holmes activities, please visit www.sweetcherrypublishing.com/resources